the MiLO & JAZZ MYSTERIES®

THE CASE OF THE CROOKEd CAMPAIGN

by Lewis B. Montgomery
illustrated by Amy Wummer

The KANE PRESS
New York

Library of Congress Cataloging-in-Publication Data

Montgomery, Lewis B.
The case of the crooked campaign / by Lewis B. Montgomery ;
illustrated by Amy Wummer.
p. cm. -- (Milo & Jazz Mysteries ; 9)
Summary: When detective-in-training Jazz runs for school president and
someone steals her best ideas, Jazz and her sleuthing partner Milo must solve the
mystery before Election Day.
ISBN 978-1-57565-435-5 (library reinforced binding) --
ISBN 978-1-57565-436-2 (pbk.) -- ISBN 978-1-57565-437-9 (e-book)
[1. Mystery and detective stories. 2. Elections--Fiction. 3. Schools--Fiction.]
I. Wummer, Amy, ill. II. Title.
PZ7.M7682Cagh 2012
[Fic]--dc23
2011048821

1 3 5 7 9 10 8 6 4 2

First published in the United States of America in 2012 by Kane Press, Inc.
Printed in the United States of America
WOZ0712

Book Design: Edward Miller

The Milo & Jazz Mysteries is a registered trademark of Kane Press, Inc.

Visit us online at **www.kanepress.com**

Like us on Facebook
facebook.com/kanepress

Follow us on Twitter
@KanePress

For the real Perkins poodles
(and their people!)
—L.B.M.

Titles in *The Milo & Jazz Mysteries* series:

THE CASE OF THE CROOKEd CAMPAIGN

CHAPTER ONE

Milo hurried down the school hallway after his friend Jazz. "You did *WHAT*?"

"I told Spencer I'd take care of Floyd while he was visiting his grandmother," Jazz said again. "What's the big deal? He's just a parrot."

Floyd, just a parrot? Milo thought. Sure. Like Batman's crazed archenemy, The Joker, was just a guy.

"Fine," Milo said. "I'll stay away from

7

your house till Spencer gets back."

"But you can't! What about our campaign meetings?" Jazz pointed to the election signup sheet taped to the wall. "I'm running for president, remember?"

"As if I could forget!" He laughed. Jazz had dragged him down to check that sheet at least three times that day.

A bunch of kids had signed up to run for the other positions—vice president, secretary, and treasurer. So far, though, Jazz's name was still the only one under PRESIDENT.

"Why do you need to campaign?" Milo asked. "No one else is running."

"Someone might sign up," she said.

"Jazz, you've been on student council three years in a row. Everybody knows you're going to be president."

Jazz had talked of nothing else for weeks. She wanted to fix every problem in the school, from dried-out markers in the art room to cafeteria pizza that tasted like, well . . . dried-out markers.

"I still need to let everyone know what I stand for," she said. "And I need YOU on my campaign team. Partners, right?"

Milo and Jazz were sleuths in training. They cracked lots of cases—aided by lessons from Dash Marlowe, world-famous private eye.

"Partners in sleuthing, sure," Milo said. "But I'm not getting pecked to pieces at a campaign meeting. That bird has it in for me!"

"I'll shut Floyd in his cage when you come over," Jazz promised. "He's got everything in there. Food, water, toys. Even a baby monitor."

"A *baby monitor*?"

"So I can hear him from downstairs," Jazz said. "You know how Spencer is. He hated to leave Floyd. He said Floyd always goes along on family car trips, but

they couldn't take him on the plane."

Someone jostled Milo's elbow—
Gordy Fletcher.

"Signing up for stupid council?" Gordy
laughed loudly, then looked at Zack
Riley to see if he thought it was funny,
too. Zack just looked the way he usually
did: bored.

"It's *student* council," Jazz told them.
"And I'm running for president."

Gordy grinned. "Whoop-de-do."

Jazz crossed her arms. "What's that
supposed to mean? It's only the most
important job in the whole school!"

"Oh, yeah?" Zack said. "I thought that
was the principal."

Gordy laughed and punched Zack's
arm. Zack ignored him.

"You know what I mean," Jazz said. "The most important *student* job."

Zack pointed his chin toward the list. "Then how come nobody signed up to run but you?"

"They know they can't beat Jazz!" Milo said.

"Oh, yeah?" Zack looked at Jazz. "You sure of that?"

"Zack, you should run for president," Gordy said. "Rule the school."

Zack shrugged. "So? I already do."

He turned away.

Then, half smiling, he turned back. "Might as well make it official, though."

He leaned over to the sign-up sheet. Under Jazz's name, he scrawled:

ZACK RILEY.

CHAPTER TWO

Jazz's campaign team met at her house after school. Along with Milo, three others had joined her team: their friend Carlos, a quiet girl named Pria, and . . . *Brooke Whitley?*

Milo was amazed. Sure, Brooke and Jazz were getting along better this year, now that Brooke's best friends, the Emilies, were in a different class.

Still . . . Brooke as a team member? Brooke liked to be number one. He wondered why she wasn't running for something herself. Had she changed that much over the summer?

Floyd sat in a cage by Jazz's window, plucking sadly at his feathers.

Carlos said, "Isn't Floyd usually a little more . . . lively?"

Lively was not the word Milo would have used. *Fiendish* was more like it.

"I think he really misses Spencer." Jazz stepped up to the cage. "Spencer will be back soon, Floyd. He just went on a trip."

Floyd eyed the children glumly. Then, faintly, he squawked, *"Ice pie."*

"Ice pie?" Milo asked.

Jazz looked puzzled.

"Spencer left a bag of Birdie Bread. He didn't mention any other treats."

Brooke plunked down in Jazz's chair.

"Okay, everybody," she announced. "Let's get this meeting started. First, we need to choose a campaign manager.

16

That's me, of course."

"You?" Carlos said. "Why you?"

Brooke looked offended. "Well, obviously it should be someone with strong organizing skills—"

Carlos snickered. "You mean somebody bossy?"

Quickly, Jazz said, "I don't need a manager. We'll all just work together."

She pulled out a sheet of paper. "Here are the rules for the campaign. It says we're not allowed to give out candy—"

Carlos groaned.

"Or any other kind of gift or bribe. And all our campaign posters have to go in a special area in the hall."

"I'm excellent at making posters," Brooke said.

Pria spoke up for the first time, softly. "I made a poster."

Brooke stared at her. "You did? Already? But—"

"Let's see it!" Jazz said.

Pria pulled the poster from her backpack and unrolled it. Brooke hung back, frowning, as the rest of the team crowded around.

"PICK JAZZ FOR PRESIDENT," Jazz read. "Wow, Pria, this is fantastic! Where did you get a picture of my face?"

"I cropped it out of our class photo," Pria explained. "I had to scan it first."

"How did you learn to make letters like that?" Milo asked.

Pria blushed. "My dad is a graphic designer. He— *Eek!*"

Jazz's pet potbellied pig, Bitsy, had wandered in and climbed into Pria's lap. Milo didn't blame her for being startled. Bitsy was little for a pig, but she still weighed well over a hundred pounds.

"Bitsy!" Jazz scolded.

From his cage, Floyd repeated, *"Bitsy! Bitsy!"*

Bitsy glanced up at him, then away.

Jazz laughed. "I think Floyd has a crush on her. When he's out of his cage, he follows her around the house. He even tried to eat out of her bowl."

"Biiiiiiiitsy!" Floyd screeched.

The pig heaved herself off Pria's lap and stalked out of the room.

"I don't think she likes him back," Carlos said.

Milo looked at the poster again. He wondered what kind of poster Zack would put up.

"I'm worried about Zack," he said.

"What do you mean?" Jazz asked.

"I think a lot of kids will vote for him because he's, you know . . . cool."

"Everyone likes Jazz, too," Pria said.

"It's not about who everybody likes," Jazz said. "It's about who cares enough to work hard and do a really good job. And that's me, not Zack!"

Milo hoped everyone would see it that way. He knew that Jazz would be a better student council president than Zack. But if Zack wanted to win—

Well, usually, whatever Zack wanted, he got.

CHAPTER THREE

Milo felt better the next morning when he saw Pria taping up her poster in the hall at school. None of the other posters looked anywhere near as good. And Zack and Gordy hadn't put one up at all.

"See?" Jazz said as they walked down the hall toward their classrooms. "Zack doesn't care about being president. He's not even going to try."

A group of girls hurried past them. "Pick Jazz for president!" one called out. The others giggled.

Jazz looked puzzled. "Um . . . thanks."

Milo's class played Spelling Soccer and then had a pop quiz. It wasn't until morning recess that Milo thought of the election again. As his class filed down the hall, the kids at the front of the line began to laugh and point.

Milo looked. It was Pria's poster. PICK JAZZ FOR PRESIDENT, it still said, beside a picture of a smiling Jazz.

But under that, someone had stuck a giant foam finger, the kind that people wave at sports events.

The finger appeared to be picking Jazz's nose.

On the playground, Jazz's campaign team huddled together.

Jazz was furious. "Everyone in school is laughing at me now!"

"It's my fault," Pria said. "I'm the one who wrote PICK JAZZ."

Milo thought he saw Brooke smile, but she turned her head away before he could be sure.

"Don't be silly," Jazz told Pria. "Everybody knows whose fault it is." She glared at Zack and Gordy, who were shooting layups. "And I'm going to give them a piece of my mind."

Jazz strode off, leaving the others staring after her. They caught up with her as she reached the basketball court.

"Are you sure this is a good idea?" Carlos asked.

"Hey! It's Team Booger!"

Gordy stood grinning, basketball under his arm.

Jazz marched straight up to Zack. "You're supposed to make your own poster," she said. "Not mess up mine."

Zack looked bored. "I don't know what you're talking about."

"Yeah!" Gordy said. "Me neither." He mimed poking his finger up his nose, and then laughed.

Jazz said to Zack, "If you think this election is a joke, you shouldn't run. Instead of making fun of me, why don't you come up with your own ideas?"

"What? Bringing in that finger was a great idea!" Gordy said.

Jazz's eyes narrowed.

Slowly, she said, "You brought that finger in to put on my poster because it said PICK JAZZ FOR PRESIDENT."

Gordy snorted. "Duh."

"But the poster just went up this morning." Jazz's hands went to her hips, and she leaned forward. *How did you know ahead of time what it would say?*

Silence.

Gordy's mouth dropped open. Even Zack looked startled.

Milo stared at them. He thought back to that morning. Those giggling girls had passed him and Jazz in the hall just after Pria had put up the poster. So Zack and Gordy *must* have been ready with the finger right away!

Zack's startled look faded and was replaced by his lazy half smile.

"How *could* anyone know?" he said.

"That's what I asked," Jazz said.

Zack gazed around the group of kids facing him. Milo. Carlos. Pria. Brooke. Then he looked back at Jazz.

"I guess somebody must have spilled the beans," he said.

Startled, Jazz turned to her team. They all shook their heads.

"Not me!"

"No way!"

"None of us would tell him anything!"

Still half-smiling, Zack shrugged. "Okay. Whatever."

Jazz's hands flew to her hips. "Are you trying to say that someone on my team is lying?"

"I'm not *trying* to say anything," Zack said.

With that, he grabbed the ball from Gordy, dribbled to the basket, and shot. The ball went in.

CHAPTER FOUR

After school, Milo hurried over to Jazz's house. He wanted to talk to her alone before the rest of the campaign team arrived.

Walking into her room, he tossed his backpack on the floor next to her bed. It landed with a thump.

"SQUAWWWWWK!"

A flurry of feathers burst out from under the bed and headed straight for Milo, murder in its eyes.

"AAAAAAAH!" Milo jumped back.
"Parrot ambush!"

Jazz scooped Floyd up and smoothed
his ruffled feathers. "Don't be silly. You
just startled him."

"What was he doing under there?"

"Oh, sometimes he wanders into a dark place and falls asleep. My mom once found him in the laundry hamper. Lucky he didn't get dumped in the washing machine!"

Hmph. As far as Milo was concerned, a run through the spin cycle might do Floyd some good.

Jazz popped the parrot in its cage, and Milo sat down on the floor.

"So, I've been thinking about who could have told Zack about the poster," Milo said.

Jazz nodded. "Yeah. Me too."

"It can't be Carlos," Milo said.

"Of course not! We've been friends forever."

"And Pria seems so nice. . . ." He paused. "Maybe a little *too* nice?"

"She *is* nice," Jazz said firmly. "Anyway, it was Pria's poster. Why would she want it messed up?"

"What about Brooke, then?" Milo asked. "She seemed pretty jealous about Pria's poster. Plus, she didn't get to be campaign manager like she wanted. And Carlos called her bossy."

Jazz frowned. "I know she was upset about that stuff. But so upset she'd turn into a spy?"

"Ice pie," Floyd said from his cage. He put his head under his wing.

"Well, then, who is the spy?" Milo asked Jazz.

"I don't think there is one," Jazz said.

"Zack was probably just trying to bug me."

Milo jumped up. "That's it!"

"That's what?"

"A bug! You know, one of those tiny things that people use to listen in." His gaze shot wildly around her room. "I bet Zack has this whole place bugged!"

Jazz rolled her eyes. "Milo, come on. We're talking about a kid our own age, not some bad guy in a movie. And Zack has never even been inside my house."

"What about Gordy? He lives right down the block."

"You seriously think I would invite *Gordy* up to my room?" Jazz shook her head.

"He could have sneaked in through

the window," Milo said.

"My room is on the second floor," Jazz reminded him.

"Well . . . has he given you anything?" Milo asked. "A bug can be disguised all kinds of ways. I saw an old TV show where a bug was hidden in a shoe."

"Who would give someone a shoe?"
Jazz said. "Anyway, I know better than to
take anything from Gordy."

She had a point. Gordy's "presents"
tended to make people itch, squirt water
in their faces, or explode.

Milo sat down on Jazz's bed. "Okay.
But if it's not a bug, then how did Zack
and Gordy find out about the poster
ahead of time?"

"Maybe they saw Pria with it on the
way over here yesterday," Jazz said.

Milo shook his head. "She had it rolled
up. Remember?"

"Well, maybe it was an accident. Like,
maybe Pria and her mom were at the
supermarket, talking, and they didn't
realize Gordy and *his* mom were in the

next aisle over. . . ."

Milo just looked at Jazz.

"Okay, it's not *that* likely," she said.
"But it's a lot more likely than my room
being bugged. Or somebody on my own
team being a spy."

"ICE PIE!" Floyd squawked.

A light dawned.

"I don't think he's saying ice pie,"
Milo said. "I think he's saying . . . *a spy*!"

Jazz shrugged. "So? He's a parrot. He's
repeating what I said."

"He said it yesterday, too!" Milo said.
"During the meeting! Do you think he
was trying to tell us something?"

"Come on, Milo. He's just a bird."

Milo looked at Floyd.

Floyd blew him a loud Bronx cheer.

Then he laughed like a hyena.

Just a bird? Milo didn't think so.

Floyd was crazy. Floyd was mean. But Floyd was very, very smart. Maybe Jazz didn't want to believe that anybody on her team could be a spy. But Milo planned to keep a close eye on the other team members during today's meeting.

And on Floyd.

CHAPTER FIVE

Pria came in with a brand-new poster she had made to replace the one Gordy and Zack had ruined. It had a big mirror sticker on it, and it said LOOK WHO'S VOTING FOR JAZZ.

Everyone clustered around to admire it, except for Brooke, who suddenly had to find something deep in her backpack.

No doubt about it, Milo thought. Brooke was not happy about Pria having all the ideas.

He glanced toward Floyd's cage, hoping for a hint. Was Brooke the spy? But Floyd was busy picking at a chunk of Birdie Bread.

Jazz wanted to talk about election day. Before the voting, every candidate would give a speech, saying what they would do for the school if they won.

Jazz had a zillion ideas—like a "book-nic," where the kids ate lunch outside and everybody brought a book, and a "world's fair," where every class made food and led activities from a different country.

But the idea the whole team liked best was the Pizza Plan. Everyone at school dreaded pizza day, because the cafeteria pizza was so bad.

"I've heard it comes out of the freezer

in big cardboard boxes," Brooke said.

"I've heard the crust is *made* from cardboard boxes," Carlos said. "And the cheese is really leftover white glue."

Jazz's plan was to get the lunch people to order pizza from Angie's instead. Angie's was the most popular pizza place in town.

"But won't it cost more?" Pria asked. "My parents are always talking about money problems at the school."

"Maybe we could have a fundraiser," Milo said.

"That's just what I was thinking!" Jazz

said. "But not the same old stuff, like getting parents to buy mugs or smelly candles. I want to do something different and fun."

The door opened, and Jazz's dad poked his head in. "Anybody hungry? My muffins just came out."

The team stampeded down the stairs and gathered around the kitchen table.

Through a mouthful of hot muffin, Carlos said, "'Ow abou' a bake shale?"

Jazz spread butter on her muffin. "The Mathletes already have a bake sale. Pee Wee Football, too."

"Makeovers!" Brooke said.

Milo and Jazz glanced at each other. Brooke always had the same idea.

Carlos groaned. "Makeovers! Yuck.

What's next, a kissing booth?" He made smoochy noises.

Brooke set her glass of milk down with a thunk.

"I wouldn't kiss *you* for a million dollars," she told Carlos. "I'd rather eat cafeteria pizza every day for the rest of my life. I'd rather—"

Looking around, she spotted Bitsy, who had followed them into the kitchen and was gazing longingly at the muffins.

"I'd rather kiss a pig!" she finished, glaring at Carlos.

He snickered. "I'd pay to see that."

A loud screech interrupted their squabble. Startled, Milo spun around. Had Floyd gotten out of his cage?

"That thing is getting on my nerves,"

Jazz's dad said. He picked up something on the counter that looked like a walkie-talkie, only pink. He clicked it off.

Oh, right. Milo had forgotten about Floyd's baby monitor. Spencer really was a nut about that bird!

Jazz was staring into space, muffin halfway to her mouth.

"Are you okay?" Milo asked.

Jazz put down the muffin. "Carlos, you're a genius!"

"I am?" Carlos said.

Jazz turned to Brooke. "And you're a genius, too!"

"What are you talking about?" Brooke demanded.

"Carlos said he'd pay to see you kiss a pig."

"So?"

Jazz smiled. "I bet lots of kids would pay to see somebody kiss a pig. Like, say . . . their teacher."

"Or the principal!" Milo said.

"We could put out money jars with people's names on them," Brooke said. "And whoever's jar got the most money, that person would have to kiss your pig. In front of the whole school!"

"Would any of the teachers do that?" Pria asked.

"Sure!" Carlos said. "For a good cause. Remember all the teachers who went in the dunking booth last spring?"

Everyone was grinning widely now. Even Brooke.

Carlos stuck his hand across the table. "Kiss a Pig!"

Jazz slapped her hand on top of his. Then Milo, Brooke, and Pria added theirs. "Kiss a pig!" they all yelled, and threw their hands up in the air.

Milo looked around at the smiling faces. How could any of them be a spy?

Maybe Jazz was right, and Zack and Gordy had found out about Pria's poster by accident somehow. In that case, there was nothing to worry about. After all, lightning never struck twice.

Did it?

CHAPTER SIX

The next morning, Milo overslept. He gulped down a quick bowl of cereal and rushed off to school. He slid into his seat just as the PA speaker finished playing the school song.

Then the principal announced, "Today we have a special message."

After a pause and some muffled sounds, another voice came on.

"This is Gordy Fletcher, campaign manager for ZACK RILEY."

Milo glanced over at Carlos.

Carlos made a gagging face.

"ZACK RILEY knows how all you little people suffer here at school," Gordy went on. "Right, ZACK?"

Zack's drawl: "Yeah, sure."

"ZACK RILEY feels your pain. Because ZACK RILEY has eaten the pizza in the cafeteria."

As giggles broke out around him, Milo felt a twinge of uneasiness.

"ZACK RILEY wants to end the suffering. ZACK RILEY wants to bring us . . . Tell them, ZACK!"

Zack came on again. "Angie's pizza."

The class exploded with cheers.

Milo and Carlos stared at each other. That was *Jazz's* plan!

"But how will we pay for this pizza?" Gordy's voice went on. "Never fear, ZACK RILEY has the answer—"

Milo held his breath. Please, no!

"—and tomorrow, on election day, you'll find out what it is!"

The principal came back on to talk about the candidate speeches and voting, but nobody paid any attention.

The class buzzed. Everyone was trying to guess how Zack planned to raise money to buy Angie's pizza.

Milo didn't have to guess.

Zack and Gordy's pizza plan was Jazz's pizza plan. If Zack and Gordy had found out about that, then they knew everything about yesterday's campaign meeting. And that included Kiss a Pig.

On the way out to recess, Milo saw that Zack and Gordy had spoiled Pria's second poster. Above LOOK WHO'S VOTING FOR JAZZ, they had stuck a picture over the mirror. It was a picture of a chimpanzee.

A slow burn crept up Milo's neck. Gordy and Zack really were making monkeys out of Jazz's campaign team! They either sabotaged or stole every idea the team came up with.

Gordy and Zack might have found out about the first poster by accident. But the second poster? And the pizza idea?

This was no accident.

In Milo's head, he heard Floyd's squawk again: *A spy!*

When he got outside, Milo saw an excited crowd surrounding Zack and Gordy. Zack leaned back, half smiling, while Gordy held forth.

Jazz's campaign team clustered on the other side of the playground.

Jazz was fuming. "I'm going right over there and telling everybody they stole our idea!"

"No one will believe you," Pria said. She looked close to tears.

Carlos agreed. "How can we prove it? Zack and Gordy will just say you're being a bad sport."

Brooke clenched her fists. "We can't let them get away with it. It isn't fair!"

Milo looked at her. She really seemed upset. It was hard to believe she could be faking.

But if Brooke wasn't the spy, who was?

"We need to figure out how Zack and

Gordy are learning our plans," Milo said. "*Someone* is giving them away."

Quickly, he scanned the others' faces, hoping to catch a flash of guilt.

Jazz frowned. "Milo—"

"He's right," Brooke said.

Everyone looked at her.

"The five of us were at the meetings," Brooke said. "Zack and Gordy weren't. So how do they keep stealing our ideas?"

"Maybe somebody told them by accident," Pria suggested. "You know, like a younger brother or sister."

Carlos shook his head. "My sisters are too little. They don't even go to school." He looked at Milo.

Milo considered. His younger brother certainly had a big mouth. But Milo was sure Ethan had no idea of their campaign plans. He shook his head, too.

"I haven't told anyone anything," Brooke said.

"Me neither," Pria said.

They all looked at each other.

"Now what?" Carlos asked.

Jazz sighed.

"I don't know," she said. "But we'd better figure out something—and soon. Otherwise, Zack is going to win this election by a landslide!"

CHAPTER SEVEN

When Milo dropped Ethan off after
school, he saw an envelope with his
name on the kitchen table.

A new lesson from Dash!

DASH MARLOWE
SECRETS OF A SUPER SLEUTH!

Relevant and Irrelevant Information

Everybody knows that clues help a detective solve a case. But all clues aren't created equal. A clue that seems important may turn out to be a **red herring**—irrelevant information that leads you away from the real solution.

I learned about red herrings in one of my very first cases. Arriving on the scene of a bank robbery, I spotted a tiny scrap of paper near the teller's window. I picked it up and found that it was a Brazilian postage stamp.

Aha! I thought. A gang of robbers from Brazil!

I slipped the stamp into my pocket, careful

not to be seen by the police detective, Captain Phil Ately. After all, I wanted to be the one to crack the case!

Hours later, my plane touched down in Brazil, and I was off. By day, I cheered at soccer matches while I scanned the crowd. By night, I danced the samba while I questioned suspects. Wherever a clue led, I followed—mountain, beach, or plains. I even paddled up the Amazon, where I saw tree frogs, howler monkeys, and electric eels . . . but no bank robbers.

At last, I gave up and returned to the United States. At an airport newsstand, I saw the headline: ROBBERS NABBED. Captain Ately had caught the bank heist gang!

I rushed to police headquarters. "Where did you track down the robbers?" I asked the captain. "Sao Paulo? Rio de Janeiro?"

He looked puzzled. "Hoboken, New Jersey."

"New Jersey! But what about this?" I pulled out the Brazilian stamp.

Captain Ately's eyes lit up. "You found it!"

he exclaimed. "I knew it must have fallen out of my pocket somewhere. This time I'll make sure it goes straight into my stamp collection!"

Yes, I learned about red herrings the hard way. But I did have a terrific tan.

Milo stuffed the lesson in his pocket and headed to Jazz's house. He found her sitting out on the front porch, writing in her detective notebook.

While Jazz read Dash's lesson, Milo looked at what she'd written.

The Case of the Crooked Campaign

Who: Zack and Gordy

What: Messing up our posters, stealing our ideas

How:

That was the question, Milo thought. *How?* How did Zack and Gordy find out whatever they planned to do?

A door slammed, and Jazz's neighbor, Mrs. Budge, strode out of her house carrying a cordless phone with the wires trailing behind.

"I'm going to do it this time," she announced. "Even if it makes me feel like a murderer."

"Do what?" Jazz asked.

Mrs. Budge walked over to them. "I'm finally getting rid of this phone," she said. "I don't mind a little static now and then. But lately— Screeches! Squawks! It's like a jungle full of parrots."

Milo and Jazz looked at each other. *Parrots?*

Jazz said, "Are you sure you're not hearing real parrot noises, Mrs. Budge? I've been parrot-sitting for my friend."

Her neighbor looked surprised. "Oh, no. I didn't hear it through the window. Those noises are definitely coming from my phone."

Jazz stared at Mrs. Budge's phone.

"Could I borrow that?" she asked. "Just for a minute?"

An instant later, Jazz vanished inside. Milo leapt for the screen door before it slammed and hurried after her.

"I don't get it," he said. "Floyd's been calling Mrs. Budge? But how did he get to the phone? Did he figure out how to break out of his cage?"

"I don't think Floyd's using the phone

at all," Jazz said, heading for the kitchen. "I should have listened to you in the first place! You were right!"

Huh? "About what?"

She stopped and turned to him. "About my room being bugged."

"So Zack and Gordy did sneak in!" Milo exclaimed.

Jazz shook her head. "They didn't have to. The bug was already there."

"But . . . how did it get in your room?" he asked, confused. "Who planted it?"

Jazz smiled. *"Me."*

CHAPTER EIGHT

Milo stared at Jazz. "You bugged your own room?"

"Not on purpose," Jazz said. She pointed to the baby monitor receiver on the kitchen counter.

Oh . . .

It was slowly starting to make sense.

"You think Mrs. Budge's phone is picking up the noises from Floyd's baby monitor?" Milo said. "That's why she's hearing parrot screeches?"

Jazz nodded. "Let's try it for ourselves and see."

She switched on the baby monitor receiver. Then she plugged Mrs. Budge's phone into the wall and turned it on. Milo leaned close as Jazz held the phone up to her ear.

They waited.

At first Milo didn't hear anything. Then he thought he heard a faint crackling sound. He leaned in closer. Was that . . . ?

"*BIIIIIIITSY!*" the phone shrieked.

Milo jumped back, rubbing his ear.

Jazz pointed at the baby monitor receiver. "It's coming out of there, too! I was right!"

"But how is that even possible?" Milo said.

"The baby monitor in Floyd's cage is like a little radio," Jazz explained. "It sends out sound signals for the receiver to pick up. And Mrs. Budge lives so close, her phone picked up the signals too!"

They unplugged the phone and ran back out to Mrs. Budge, whose puzzled look quickly turned to a wide smile as she listened to Jazz's explanation.

"Poor old phone! So all that squawking wasn't your fault after all." Mrs. Budge patted the phone fondly. "And here I was ready to toss you out!"

"Sorry about the noise," Jazz said. "But Spencer will be home tomorrow night."

"Oh, I don't mind," Mrs. Budge said.

"Now that I know it's a real parrot!"

She thanked Jazz and left, but Milo barely noticed. His mind was in a whirl.

Floyd's baby monitor was in his cage. The cage was in Jazz's room. And Jazz's room was where they had been having their campaign meetings.

"So that's how Zack and Gordy have been spying!" Milo exclaimed. "They're hearing the sounds from Floyd's monitor, just like Mrs. Budge did!"

Jazz nodded. "I think they must be sneaking around in my yard with some kind of receiver. Another baby monitor, a walkie-talkie . . ."

"Walkie-talkies!" Milo said. "Gordy has a set of those. Remember last Halloween, how he hid one of them under a pile of leaves and tried to scare people with banshee screams when they walked by?"

"And then he ran out of his house crying when the Perkins' poodle lifted its leg on the pile of leaves," Jazz said.

Milo laughed. "Served him right."

Another question popped into his head.

"But how did Zack and Gordy know there was a baby monitor in Floyd's cage?"

Jazz frowned. "Maybe they heard us talking about it at school?"

Milo thought back. "That's right! They were in the hall when you told me. Remember? That was when Zack signed up to run for president."

Jazz scowled. "Even though he doesn't have a single good idea for the school!"

"He doesn't need his own ideas," Milo said. "He's got ours."

Jazz sighed. Then her eyes widened. "Or . . . does he?"

"What do you mean? Didn't you hear him get on the PA this morning and tell everyone about Angie's pizza?"

"I didn't hear him say anything about Kiss a Pig," Jazz said.

"He's saving it for the assembly," Milo reminded her.

"Maybe he just said that," Jazz said. "Maybe he really doesn't know what our fundraising idea is."

"But he heard our whole campaign meeting!"

Jazz lifted an eyebrow. "Even when *we went down to the kitchen?*"

Holy cow. She was right!

Floyd's monitor only picked up sounds made near his cage. Once they'd left Jazz's room, nothing they said could have been overheard.

"So Zack and Gordy *don't* know about Kiss a Pig!" Milo exclaimed.

"Not yet, anyway," Jazz said. "They're probably counting on hearing us talk about our big idea today."

Milo grinned. "But we'll have the monitor turned off this time, and they won't hear a thing."

"Oh, yes they will," Jazz said.

"Huh?"

Jazz smiled.

"We're going to have a very special campaign meeting today," she said. "And we want Zack and Gordy to hear every word."

CHAPTER NINE

It took a while to explain everything
to the team. After Jazz told them about
the spying, Brooke wanted to march
right over to Zack's house and give him
a piece of her mind. Pria ran to the
bathroom and came back with a red
nose. And Carlos just kept muttering,
"Those *rats*!"

Finally, though, everyone settled
down to listen to Jazz's plan.

"We'll let them hear our meeting," Jazz said, holding up the monitor which she had taken from Floyd's cage. It was turned off for now. "Only it won't be a real meeting. It'll be a fake. We'll all have lines, just like a play."

Pria chewed her lip. "I've never done anything like that before."

"I'm excellent at acting," Brooke announced.

"That's great! Would you help me?" Pria asked.

Brooke looked startled. "Well . . . sure. I guess."

Pria smiled at her gratefully. After a moment, Brooke smiled back.

"But what are we going to say?" Carlos asked.

"We're going to talk about how we can't wait for the assembly," Jazz said. "How we're dying to see Zack and Gordy's faces when we open the box."

Everyone spoke at once. "The box?" "What box?"

Jazz smiled. "The box Gordy and Zack are going to steal."

"But . . . what's in the box?" Pria asked.

"Nothing," Jazz said.

Carlos shook his head. "I don't get it. Why would they steal an empty box?"

"They won't know that it's empty," Jazz explained. "They'll think there's something in it—a super-secret surprise that's going to win the election."

Milo chimed in. "Gordy and Zack

promised to tell kids their idea to raise money for pizza. But they're counting on overhearing *our* idea at today's meeting, and then passing it off as their own."

"So we'll pretend we have an election-winning surprise in the box," Jazz continued. "We'll say we plan to open the box at the assembly. When Zack and Gordy hear that, they'll steal the box, open it themselves in front of everyone, and find their big surprise—*nothing*!"

Brooke frowned. "But what if they don't steal the box?"

"Yeah," Carlos said. "What if they guess it's a trick?"

Jazz shrugged. "Then Zack still has to explain how he's planning to raise money for pizza. And if his idea beats ours, then

Zack wins the election fair and square.

"Uh-uh!" "No way!" the others yelled.

"But since they haven't even tried to come up with their own ideas," she went on, "I bet they'll steal the box. Zack won't be able to resist it when he sees it sitting on the stage."

Pria spoke up. "Won't that only work if Zack goes first, instead of you?"

"Zack's going first," Jazz assured her. "The principal called all the student council candidates into his office yesterday and flipped a coin."

Milo had to admit that Jazz always thought of everything. It sounded like a foolproof plan.

Bitsy wandered into the room and climbed into Pria's lap. Pria petted her.

"BIIIIITSY!" Floyd called from his cage.

Shooting Floyd an offended glance, Bitsy heaved herself back to her feet and left.

"BIIIIIIIITSY!" Floyd called after her. *"BIIIIIIIIIIIIIIIIIIIIIIIIIIITSY!"*

While the team practiced their lines, Carlos stood by the window as lookout. Suddenly he said, "They're here!"

Jazz smiled. Flipping on the monitor, she said, "Okay. Let's get this meeting under way."

It all went pretty smoothly. Brooke flubbed a line, but Jazz covered for her by quickly coming up with a new line of her own. Pria managed to squeak out her part without any slip-ups.

When the "meeting" was over, they all said their goodbyes and noisily went out the door. Then, quietly, they crept back in.

Milo and Jazz tiptoed to the window. A bush in the backyard was quivering. Suddenly, two figures dashed out from behind it. As Gordy and Zack ran across the yard, Milo spotted a walkie-talkie in Zack's hand.

Jazz switched off the monitor and gave the rest of the team the thumbs-up. They cheered.

Milo sucked in a deep breath. The first part of their plan had gone perfectly.

But what would happen tomorrow at the assembly?

CHAPTER TEN

The election-day assembly was more than
halfway over. Milo, crouched deep in the
stage wing, listened to a younger boy drone
on about why he should be elected vice
president.

". . . and I'm respectful. And honest.
And kind. And caring. And fair . . ."

Bitsy grunted impatiently.

Milo tightened his hand around her
leash. "I'm bored too," he whispered. "But

we have to wait for Jazz's turn."

He still couldn't believe Jazz had decided to bring Bitsy to the assembly at the last second. Okay, sure, it would be fun to announce Kiss a Pig with a real pig. But keeping Bitsy hidden until then? Not so fun.

Milo peeked around the curtain again. Jazz and Zack sat in the front row with the other student council candidates.

Further back, he spotted Pria, Brooke, and Carlos sitting together.

". . . and trustworthy. And helpful . . ."

A large cardboard box sat in the opposite wing. Jazz had carefully placed it so it wasn't *too* well hidden.

The kid at the microphone finished at last, and the principal called Zack's name.

As Zack came up onstage, he peered into the wings. Milo pulled Bitsy further back. But Zack wasn't looking at them. His eyes were on the box. His mouth was twisted in a half-smile.

Zack stepped up to the microphone. "I'm not going to tell you about myself,"

he said. "I don't have to."

There were cheers from the students. Milo peeked out again. In the front row, Jazz sat with her arms crossed. Her face was stony.

"All you want to know is how we're going to raise pizza money," Zack said. "Right?"

More cheers.

"Okay, then. Gordy, come on up."

Gordy squeezed out of his row and bounded up onstage. When he saw the box in the wings, he grinned. He picked it up and carried it out to Zack.

The audience waited in eager silence.

Zack lifted one flap, then another—

SQUAWKKKKKK!

A flurry of bright color burst out of the box into Zack's face. Zack yelled and jumped backward. He tripped and fell.

Milo leaned out from the wings.

Floyd?

Wheeling around, Floyd landed on Gordy's curly hair. Screaming, Gordy batted at his head, but Floyd dug in his claws.

"BIIIIIIIIIIIIIIIITSY!"

Bitsy's small eyes focused on her unwelcome admirer. She had taken all a pig could stand. With a grunt of rage, she charged.

The leash snapped out of Milo's hand. Seeing Bitsy bearing down on him, Floyd lifted off from Gordy's head. As Bitsy trampled Gordy, Floyd flew into Zack, who was just trying to sit up. Zack hit the floor again.

The auditorium was in total chaos. Jazz ran up onto the stage, followed by Carlos, Brooke, and Pria.

"Bitsy!" Jazz yelled. "Floyd!"

Milo dove for Bitsy's leash and missed. Brooke and Carlos, both running toward Floyd, crashed into each other. Floyd flapped away.

"QUIET!"

Instantly, the auditorium fell silent. The principal stood at the microphone, glaring out at the students.

"Please return to your seats. NOW."

He turned to the frozen scene onstage. Pria had her arms flung around Bitsy. Milo, Brooke, and Carlos lay sprawled on the floor. Zack and Jazz stood glowering at each other.

The only movement was from Floyd. He perched on Gordy's head, calmly using his talons to comb Gordy's curls.

The principal crossed his arms. "Could someone please tell me what is going on?"

Everyone began talking at once.

"I didn't mean—"

"The box—"

"It's *their* fault. They—"

"QUIET!" the principal bellowed again. He looked at Zack. "You first. What are these animals doing at school?"

Zack pointed to Jazz. "Ask her!"

"I—I brought Bitsy," Jazz admitted.
"But I have no idea how Floyd got here!
He must have sneaked into the empty
box and gone to sleep!"

Gordy stared at her. He seemed to have forgotten the parrot on his head. "Empty box? You mean there wasn't any super-secret fundraising idea?"

"Sure there was," Carlos said. "That's what the pig is for."

"A pig in a box?" Gordy asked.

Carlos looked confused. "Why would we put a pig in a box?"

The principal held up his hand. "Enough!" He turned to Jazz. "Let me get this straight. *You* brought that box to school?"

"See? It's all their fault!" Zack said.

The principal pinned him with a look. "And why, exactly, were you opening a box that your opponent's campaign team brought in?"

Zack's mouth opened. Then it closed. No sound came out.

"I can explain," Jazz said.

The auditorium fell silent as Jazz stepped up to the microphone. First, she told about Zack and Gordy's spying and how she and her team had set a trap. Then she told about Kiss a Pig and all her other ideas for the school.

"And so," she concluded, "even though things didn't go *exactly* right today—"

Everyone laughed.

"I hope you'll still vote for me. Because this school needs a president with good ideas—of her *own*."

The auditorium filled with cheers.

CHAPTER ELEVEN

Monday at lunch, Jazz and Milo set out
money jars on a table. Behind them, Pria
and Brooke hung a giant poster they had
made together. It said WHO WILL KISS
THE PIG?

Carlos and Spencer stopped by the
table. While Carlos checked out the
names on the jars, Milo asked Spencer,
"How was your plane trip?"

"I liked takeoff and landing," Spencer said. "But in between was sort of boring. Nothing to see but clouds. On car trips, Floyd and I look out the window and see lots of stuff. We play I Spy."

Jazz and Milo stared at him.

Milo repeated, "*I Spy?*"

"You know, like, 'I spy with my little eye . . . something green!'" Spencer said. "You never played that on a car trip?"

"Yeah," Milo said glumly. "I have."

So that was what Floyd had been saying! He didn't know anything about "a spy." He just knew Spencer had gone on a trip, and he wished he'd been taken along.

Now *there* was a red herring to tell Dash about. Milo had been so sure that Floyd could lead them to the spy!

"I wish I'd gotten back in time to vote for you," Spencer told Jazz.

Jazz smiled. "That's okay. I won anyway."

"By a landslide!" Carlos held up his hand for a high five. Milo and Jazz both slapped it.

Spencer looked over at Zack and Gordy on the other side of the cafeteria. They were eating alone.

"I bet Zack still can't believe he lost," Spencer said.

Jazz said, "Well, now he's got another chance to win something."

"What do you mean?" Spencer asked.

Jazz pointed to a jar labeled "ZACK RILEY."

"Zack volunteered to kiss a pig?"

Milo laughed. "He *got* volunteered— by the principal."

"I never thought I'd vote for Zack," Carlos said, pulling a dollar from his pocket and putting it in the jar.

Milo knew exactly how he felt. Nothing would make him happier than seeing Zack win this competition.

Fair and square.

SUPER SLEUTHING STRATEGIES

A few days after Milo and Jazz wrote to Dash Marlowe, a letter arrived in the mail. . . .

Greetings, Milo and Jazz,

Congrats! Another bang-up detecting job on a tough case—and you managed to win an election while you were at it!

Floyd may have been a red herring in this case, but I still say "Never underestimate the power of a parrot." One day I'll have to tell you about The Case of the Bossy Bird. . . .

Happy Sleuthing!
—*Dash Marlowe*

Warm Up!
Here are a few brain stretchers to warm you up. (The answers to these and the other sleuthing puzzles are at the end of my letter.)

1. If your own uncle's sister is not your aunt, then what is your relationship to her?
2. A clerk in a butcher shop is five foot ten. What does he weigh?
3. Before Mount Everest was discovered, what was the highest mountain in the world?
4. What came first, the chicken or the egg?

Spot the Difference: An Observation Puzzle

Dirty tricks aren't just confined to school elections! Not long ago a client, Jeff Jarvis, who was running for city mayor, told me that a newspaper had run a photo that *seemed* to show him making a payoff to a known criminal! Of course, the photo was a fake—someone from his rival's campaign had pasted Jeff's head on another man's body. Luckily it was a sloppy job. Take a look at the two photos and try to spot the differences between the fake Jeff and the real one! (I showed the two photos to the paper and they printed an apology.)

Con Campaign: A Logic Puzzle

Back when ex-robbers Louie, Sal, and Rocky were in prison, there was so much fighting on their cellblock that the convicts decided they should elect an inmate to be Big Boss. The three friends all ran for the job. Can you figure out who of the three guys had which slogan and how each guy did in the race?

Look at the clues and fill in the answer box where you can. Then read the clues again to find the answer.

Answer Box (answers at end of letter)

	Rocky	Louie	Sal
Slogan			
Place			

1. Rocky's slogan was BEST TATTOO ON CELLBLOCK 9. He promised everybody a free tattoo if he won.
2. Sal came in second to last.
3. The one who got the fewest votes gave away broccoli-flavored chewing gum.
4. One robber's posters said VOTE FOR ME—OR ELSE!
5. Louie's slogan was WHY DON'T CHEW VOTE FOR ME?

Something Fishy: A Mini-Mystery

"Red herrings" reminded me of this quirky case. Give it a try—and draw a conclusion!

A daring masked man had robbed a local bank. Police had trailed him to a nearby lake where it would be easy for the culprit to lose himself among the fishermen lining its shore. I was called in to help find him. I started by approaching three men on the dock and asking each one, "Did you see anybody show up here within the last hour?"

"I'm afraid I was asleep," the first man said. "For me, fishing is an excuse for a nice nap. To tell you the truth, I don't even bait my hook!"

The second man told me, "I was busy battling a scrappy little fish." He chuckled. "Then when I finally landed him he looked so pathetic—eyes closed, gasping for breath—that I threw him back!"

The third smiled, "I wasn't paying much attention. I was scoping out a pretty girl water skiing. I think she's interested. She waved at me!"

All three stories sounded pretty suspicious. But I knew one of them contained a lie. Which was it?

Yada Yada: A Relevant/Irrelevant Puzzle

A witness can really help a detective solve crimes. But witnesses can also tell you lots of things you don't need to know. Check out some of the things witnesses have told me. See if you can spot the irrelevant information a detective should ignore! (Remember: An irrelevant comment can be perfectly true; it just won't help you find out what you want to know.)

1. I was hired by the owner of Pizza Pronto to catch whoever kept painting "YUCK! DON'T EAT HERE!" on the restaurant door. A customer said he might know who did it. This is what he told me:

   a. Pizza Pronto stays open late.
   b. The food is fabulous, especially the meatballs.
   c. A place called Pizza Plus is across the street.
   d. The parking meter in front of Pizza Pronto is broken.
   e. The guy who owns Pizza Plus had paint in his hair.

2. My 8-year-old neighbor, Pete, was very angry. "I went to get more milk during lunch—and somebody took a bite out of my tuna sandwich!" His friend Owen broke in, "I'm not sure who did it, but I was at the same table." Here's what Owen told me:

   a. Joey sat next to Pete and he loves tuna sandwiches.

b. Karen sat next to Frank and she likes tuna too.

c. Frank sat across from Pete but he loves peanut butter, not tuna.

d. Joey's breath smelled like tuna.

e. I like cheese sandwiches.

3. Mrs. Wilson's brand new computer was stolen from her house in broad daylight. Her neighbor reported:

a. I saw a guy in uniform knock on the front door, then go around to the back.

b. I'd been watching reality TV.

c. He came out carrying something wrapped in newspapers.

d. He stopped for a second to scrape something off his shoe.

e. He had a green and white van with lots of dents.

4. Just before closing time a woman burst into the Devastating Beauty Salon and said, "This is a stick-up!" Five minutes later she left with all the cash in the register. I asked Madame Cherie, the only one there at the time, to describe the robber. She said:

a. Her cut wasn't flattering.

b. She was tall and had short bleached blond hair.

c. I wouldn't be surprised if she cut her hair herself.

d. I'm sure she used a very cheap shampoo.

e. Probably no conditioner either.

Super Sleuthing Answers!

Answers to Brain Stretchers:
1. She is your own mother.
2. Meat.
3. Mount Everest was the highest, even before it was discovered!
4. The egg. (Dinosaurs laid eggs long before there were chickens!)

Answer to Observation Puzzle: The man in the fake photo has a tattoo on his arm, hairy arms, a pot belly, dark chest hair showing at his shirt opening, a scar on his neck, and he wears no rings. Jeff has no tattoo, no hairy arms, no pot belly, no dark chest hair, no scar, and he wears a ring.

Answer to Logic Puzzle: Sal's slogan was VOTE FOR ME—OR ELSE. Since he came in second to last, it must not have scared anybody.

Louie came in last. The cons liked the broccoli-flavored chewing gum but they hated his slogan, WHY DON'T CHEW VOTE FOR ME. Rocky won! He was busy doing free tattoos for months.

Answer to Mini Mystery: I knew the second guy was not a fisherman when he said the fish he caught had its eyes closed. Fish can't close their eyes! Sure enough, after a bit of grilling, he confessed to being the robber.

Answers to Relevant/Irrelevant Puzzle:
1. a., b., and d. are not relevant. But c. is—and yep, e. pointed me right to the culprit, the jealous owner of Pizza Plus.
2. Only e. is totally irrelevant. Tuna breath was the real giveaway. (Joey admitted he took the bite. "I had baloney and I just wasn't in the mood!" He gave Pete a cookie to make up for it.)
3. b. and d. are irrelevant. I caught the guy after I checked for owners of green and white vans with bad driving records.
4. b. was helpful, but only another hair stylist would care about the rest. The blonde was caught after she held up several other salons.

Don't miss book #10 in
The Milo & Jazz Mysteries:

The Case of the Superstar Scam

When teen idol Starr Gonzalez comes to Westview to
film an episode of her hit TV show, *Super Starr*, the
entire town is abuzz—especially Jazz's big brother
Chris and his superfan friends! But when kids start
receiving mysterious letters from "Starr" asking them
to hand over their valuable show memorabilia, Milo
and Jazz suspect one thing: a super *scam*! Can the two
detectives-in-training get to the bottom of the case
before any more kids are swindled?

COMING SOON
More mysteries from your favorite kid detectives!

www.kanepress.com/miloandjazz.html

#4: The Case of the Amazing Zelda

Is the pet psychic truly as amazing as she seems?
". . . most definitely lives up to the high quality of its
predecessors . . . fun page-turner . . . would make a great
addition to elementary school and public libraries."
—*Library Media Connection*

#5: The Case of the July 4th Jinx

2011 Moonbeam Children's Book Award Silver Medal Winner
Is the fair jinxed . . . or is it a case of *sabotage*?
"Quick paced, humorous, kid friendly . . . excellent
summer reading for kids." —*Midwest Book Review*

#6: The Case of the Missing Moose

Milo's team mascot mysteriously disappears at camp.
"Engaging . . . Fun pen-and-ink illustrations enhance the story.
Numerous clues are provided, a red herring is present, and the
mystery has a surprising twist at the end. . . ." —*Booklist*

#7: The Case of the Purple Pool

Milo and Jazz investigate their most colorful case yet!
"The two youngsters are stumped when the pool water turns
purple. How? Why? . . . Young readers might just have to
exercise their brains to solve this one. I think mystery fans
ages 6–10 will enjoy this series." —*Semicolon blog*

#8: The Case of the Diamonds in the Desk

A diamond necklace? In Milo's *desk*?
"Sprightly illustrations enliven the brief
chapters, which are filled with earnest, clever
kids being funny—and, more importantly,
smart. As always, the book ends with
a series of highly enjoyable brain
teasers." —*Booklist*

Collect these mysteries
and more—coming soon!

**Visit www.kanepress.com
to see all titles in
The Milo & Jazz Mysteries.**

ABOUT THE AUTHOR

Lewis B. Montgomery is the pen name of a writer whose favorite authors include CSL, EBW, and LMM. Those initials are a clue—but there's another clue, too. Can you figure out their names?

Besides writing the Milo & Jazz mysteries, LBM enjoys eating spicy Thai noodles and blueberry ice cream, riding a bike, and reading. Not all at the same time, of course. At least, not anymore. But that's another story. . . .

ABOUT THE ILLUSTRATOR

Amy Wummer has illustrated more than 50 children's books. She uses pencils, watercolors, and ink—but not the invisible kind.

Amy and her husband, who is also an artist, live in Pennsylvania . . . in a mysterious old house which has a secret hidden room in the basement!